W9-CJM-514

SPORTS STARS

MICHAEL JORDAN

BEYOND AIR

By Philip Brooks

CHILDRENS PRESS®
CHICAGO

Photo Credits

Cover, ©Scott Wachter/Sports Photo Masters, Inc.; 5, ©Brian Drake/ Sportschrome East/West; 6, ©Tim Defrisco/Allsport; 8, 10, Reuter/ Bettmann; 11, 12, AP/Wide World; 14, ©Jonathan Kirn/Sports Photo Masters, Inc.; 16, 17, 18, 21, UPI/Bettmann; 23, AP/Wide World; 24, Reuter/Bettmann; 27, UPI/Bettmann; 29, AP/Wide World; 30, ©Noren Trotman/Sports Photo Masters, Inc.; 33, UPI/Bettmann; 34, ©Ken Levine/Allsport; 36, UPI/Bettmann; 38, ©Brian Drake/Sportschrome East/West; 39, Reuter/Bettmann; 41, Bettmann; 42, AP/Wide World; 47, Reuter/Bettmann

Project Editor: Mark Friedman
Design: Herman Adler Design Group
Photo Editor: Jan Izzo

Library of Congress Cataloging-in-Publication Data

Brooks, Philip, 1963–
Michael Jordan : beyond Air / by Philip Brooks.
p. cm. – (Sports stars)
ISBN 0-516-04391-9
1. Jordan, Michael, 1963– —Juvenile literature. 2. Basketball players—United States—Biography—Juvenile literature. 3. Chicago Bulls (Basketball team)—Juvenile literature. [1. Jordan, Michael, 1963– . 2. Basketball players. 3. Afro-Americans—Biography. 4. Chicago Bulls (Basketball team)] I. Title. II. Title: Beyond Air. III. Series.
GV884.J67B76 1995
796.323'092–dc20 94-24336
[B] CIP
AC

Printed in the United States of America.
1 2 3 4 5 6 7 8 9 10 R 04 03 02 01 00 99 98 97 96 95

MICHAEL JORDAN
BEYOND AIR

☆ ☆ ☆

June 27, 1993. Michael Jordan watched John Paxson's three-point shot swish through the net. Michael raised his fists in the air with glee. The Chicago Bulls had won their third National Basketball Association championship in a row. Michael won the Most Valuable Player award for the NBA Finals. He was the best basketball player in the world on the best team in the world. He was a very rich man who was admired by millions of people. He probably felt like the luckiest man on earth.

August 3, 1993 — just five weeks later. Something terrible happened that turned Michael Jordan's world upside down. He learned that his father, James Jordan, had been murdered by two young men who were trying to steal his money and car.

James Jordan was Michael's very best friend. They played golf together and talked about basketball and baseball. When his father died so suddenly and so brutally, Michael was sadder than he had ever been in his life.

Michael Jordan surprised the nation by announcing his retirement from basketball on October 6, 1993.

★ ★ ★

October 6, 1993. After weeks of mourning for his father, Michael announced he was retiring from basketball. Playing ball did not mean as much to him since his father would not be in the stands to share in his glory.

Jordan's announcement stunned the Chicago Bulls, Bulls' fans, and people around the world. Michael was possibly the greatest professional athlete of all time. He was 31 years old and physically healthy. He was still at the peak of his skills. Never before had such a superstar simply walked away from his career.

Michael Jordan then slipped out of the spotlight for the first time in his adult life. But people did not believe he would stay away for long. And on February 8, 1994, he returned to the public eye. He announced that he wanted to fulfill a lifelong dream and become a baseball player. The Chicago White Sox said they would invite Michael to spring training and let him try out for the team.

Again, the sports world was in shock. Not many professional athletes have succeeded in two major sports. Could the world's greatest basketball player suddenly become a major-league baseball player? A lot of people said Michael was making a mistake because he'd embarrass himself in baseball. Michael admitted they might be right, but that was okay. "I can accept failure," he said, "but I can't accept not trying."

Michael signs his minor-league contract with the White Sox as Sox vice president Ron Shueler (left) looks on.

Michael signed his baseball contract in the dead of winter, but he wanted to prove to people that he knew how to play baseball. So he went to a Chicago gym and showed off his fielding and batting skills for reporters.

Michael celebrating a birthday with his parents, James (right) and Delores (center) Jordan. Michael sees a lot of his parents' qualities in himself. He says, "My personality and my laughter come from my father; my business and serious side come from my mother."

☆ ☆ ☆

Michael Jordan was born on February 17, 1963. He grew up with two brothers and two sisters. He and his brother Larry spent a lot of time playing basketball when they were kids. Larry was older and bigger. Michael learned from him how to play hard and maintain a tough personality on the court. In high school, Michael grew to over six feet tall and towered over Larry by several inches. Larry soon could not compete with his "little" brother.

Michael had many of the same problems other kids have. He thought he was ugly, for instance. His body was extremely long and skinny, and his ears stuck out. "A lot of guys picked on me . . . they would joke about my haircut and the way I played with my tongue out." Michael's habit of playing with his tongue out came from watching his father working around the house. When his dad concentrated on a hard task, like

fixing the family car, he stuck out his tongue. Michael did the same thing when he concentrated on a lightning-fast drive to the basket.

When Michael first tried out for his high-school basketball team, he didn't make the cut. He was upset, but he didn't give up. He worked hard every day to improve his game and eventually made the team. Michael was a good player through the first two years of his high-school career. Then one summer, he went to a basketball camp, and he began to take the game seriously. He later said, "It was as though somebody tapped me on the shoulder with a magic wand and said, 'You must emerge as somebody — somebody to be admired, to achieve big things.'"

☆ ☆ ☆

From then on, Michael worked even harder and put together an impressive high-school career. But after his senior year, he was not even ranked among the top 300 prospects in the country! Michael desperately wanted to earn a basketball scholarship so he could attend a good college. Although every other school turned Michael down, Dean Smith, the coach at the University of North Carolina, decided to give Michael a chance. It was a decision Coach Smith never regretted.

In Michael's first year in college, he joined a team that already included future NBA stars James Worthy and Sam Perkins. But it was the freshman, Michael, who wound up the hero in the 1982 NCAA championship game. Facing the Georgetown Hoyas, North Carolina trailed by one point with seconds remaining. In their final time-out, Dean Smith chose Michael to take the final shot — not the older and more experienced Perkins or Worthy. Michael got the ball, moved to the baseline, jumped in the air, and fired a perfect shot. The ball swished through the net to win the national championship for the Tar Heels. Michael's play became known as "The Shot" across North Carolina. From then on, he was a national star.

Michael goes airborne and takes "The Shot" that won the 1982 NCAA championship game.

Playing for North Carolina coach Dean Smith (right), Michael learned the fundamentals of basketball.

In the next two years, Michael continued to work hard on his game, learning the fundamentals from Dean Smith. In his pro career, Michael was known as a high scorer, but in college he did not score nearly as much. Yet Michael does not think that Coach Smith held him back. “He taught me the game,” Michael says. “He taught me the importance of fundamentals and how to apply them to my individual skills. That’s what made me a complete player.”

Michael goes to the hoop in his rookie season with the Bulls.

☆ ☆ ☆

Michael left North Carolina after his third year and entered the 1984 NBA Draft. New York chose Patrick Ewing with the first pick, and Portland then drafted Sam Bowie. The Chicago Bulls, choosing third, grabbed Michael Jordan. It was a choice that would turn the Bulls from a mediocre franchise into the NBA's greatest team in decades. But even at the draft, nobody knew just how good Michael would be. One Bulls official actually warned fans not to expect too much scoring from Michael!

Michael's rookie season was both exciting and difficult. He was so popular that the fans elected him to the Eastern Conference starting team in the All-Star Game — a rare honor for a rookie. Some veteran players were not happy that a player so young and inexperienced was taking attention away from them. So in the All-Star Game, several of his teammates refused to pass the ball to Michael. He managed only seven points in the game.

☆ ☆ ☆

Michael found his rookie season difficult in other ways. The 1984–85 Bulls were not a good team. There were other talented players on the team, but none shared Michael's burning commitment to winning. Michael once went to a postgame party hosted by a teammate. Some of the other players were drunk, or were using drugs. This disgusted Michael. How could professional athletes treat their bodies that way? Why didn't they care about winning? Although his team finished poorly in his first year, Michael scored 28.2 points per game and was named NBA Rookie of the Year.

Everyone was excited about Michael's second season. Was his rookie season a fluke, or could he get even better? But in the third game of the season, Michael landed wrong on his foot and broke a tiny bone. For the first time in his life, Michael was injured severely enough to keep him from playing.

Michael brought a graceful style of play to the NBA that made him an instant star.

★ ★ ★

In the following weeks, Michael grew to hate sitting on the bench, especially because the Bulls were playing so poorly without him. After missing 64 games, Michael was anxious to get back on the court. So he ignored the advice of team doctors and started playing again. Like magic, the Bulls began winning! They managed to make the last playoff spot in their conference.

The Bulls were then crushed in a three-game sweep by the Boston Celtics, but Michael put on a spectacular one-man show. He averaged 43.7 points, including an incredible 63 points in one game. Boston's Larry Bird said, "No question he had control of the game. . . . As hard as it is to believe, it's actually fun playing against a guy like that."

Michael tangles with Boston's Larry Bird in the 1986 playoffs.

Michael's fame spread around the world. Even in Spain (above), he was a larger-than-life superstar.

☆ ☆ ☆

Jordan's Bulls were first-round playoff losers, but Michael's fame began to skyrocket. He quickly became the most popular athlete in the country. He endorsed many products, and was known worldwide for his commercials for Nike sneakers. He earned huge sums of money and played in front of sold-out crowds wherever the Bulls went. Yet Michael remained a humble person. Everyone loved his smile, and he genuinely seemed to enjoy talking to the fans. He appeared at numerous charity events, and he became a role model for millions of kids. The African-American community felt especially proud of Michael. He was a hero to kids, and he was more than just a good athlete — he was a good person, as well.

☆ ☆ ☆

In 1987–88, Michael established himself as the single best player in the NBA. He was no longer just a great scorer. He had also become the best defensive player in the game — he led the league with 259 steals! Michael took home virtually every possible award: NBA Most Valuable Player, NBA Defensive Player of the Year, All-NBA first team, NBA All-Defensive first team, All-Star Game MVP. And in the playoffs, Michael finally pushed the Bulls past the first round. His shocking, last-second jump shot eliminated the Cleveland Cavaliers. For Bulls fans, *this* shot became known as "The Shot."

Opposite Page: In 1988, Michael won his second consecutive All-Star Game slam-dunk contest.

EXIT

★ ★ ★

The Bulls advanced to the second round of the 1988 playoffs, but they were eliminated by the Detroit Pistons. Despite Michael's incredible performance, the Bulls still were not a championship team. The Pistons, nicknamed the "Bad Boys," won through intimidation on the court. They shoved, tripped, elbowed, and started fights with the Bulls. Detroit coach Chuck Daly also devised a defensive scheme called "the Jordan rules." Whenever Michael Jordan got the ball on offense, two or three Pistons would surround him. This defense succeeded in both disrupting the Bulls' offense and tiring Michael. Detroit eliminated Chicago from the playoffs in three straight seasons (1988–1990).

Michael and his wife, Juanita

Off the court, however, Michael was able to forget about winning or losing basketball games. He married Juanita Vanoy in 1989. They eventually had three children — two boys and a girl. Juanita Jordan helps Michael manage his business affairs and is the person he trusts most.

As much as Michael loved Juanita and his children, they could not help him on the court. And Michael still had one major goal to achieve in basketball: to win an NBA title.

Bulls coach Phil Jackson (center) brought a fresh approach to the Chicago offense.

☆ ☆ ☆

By the late 1980s, Michael had grown accustomed to doing everything on the court and relying on nobody else. But the Bulls had built a strong team around him. Scottie Pippen and Horace Grant were maturing and becoming All-Stars. The Bulls acquired Bill Cartwright, a veteran center who could control the lane. In 1989, new Bulls head coach Phil Jackson began convincing Michael that he must put more trust in his "supporting cast." Michael agreed to try the "Triangle Offense." This game plan emphasized passing the ball to the open man, rather than sending Michael to the hoop so often. The new system worked, and the Bulls skyrocketed to the top of the NBA.

☆ ☆ ☆

In the 1991 Eastern Conference Finals, the Bulls destroyed the rival Detroit Pistons in a four-game sweep. After years of frustration, the Bulls finally had crushed their bitter rivals. In the closing seconds of the last game, Isiah Thomas led the Pistons off the court quietly so they would not have to congratulate the new conference champions. But Michael and the Bulls did not care. They were going to the finals! They had come together as a team.

In Chicago's first trip to the NBA Finals, Magic Johnson and the Los Angeles Lakers proved no match for the Bulls. The series lasted just five games. Jordan, Pippen, Grant, and Paxson all played flawless basketball and dominated the Lakers on both offense and defense. A tired Magic Johnson said, "This is like a nightmare. I never dreamed that this would happen. I never thought about us being dominated like this."

On both defense and offense, Michael smothered Magic Johnson and his Lakers in the 1991 NBA Finals.

☆ ☆ ☆

After clinching the first NBA championship in Bulls' history, Michael Jordan sat in the locker room and hugged the golden trophy. With his parents and wife at his side, Michael sobbed with joy. After years of backbreaking work, he had

Michael in tears, clutching the NBA championship trophy

★ ★ ★

achieved his ultimate goal. The Bulls had become a great team, and Michael had become a true leader. He had learned to be more supportive of his teammates. He learned that without Pippen, Grant, Paxson, and Cartwright, Michael could not have become a world champion.

Suddenly, Michael grew more famous than ever. In the following months, the public attention on his life became a nuisance. There were times when he just wanted everyone to leave him alone. A controversy erupted when Michael did not join the Bulls on a trip to the White House for a ceremony with the president. Some people thought Michael was being disrespectful to the president. But Michael felt he needed private time with his family. He was tired of being in the spotlight.

Michael's favorite place to relax is on the golf course.

☆ ☆ ☆

Another controversy arose because Michael liked to bet money when he played golf. Some people thought he bet too much. Others objected because they thought it wrong for a children's role model to take part in gambling. Michael was angry. He believed people wanted too much from him. He enjoyed golf and had fun playing for money. He thought it was nobody's business what he did for pleasure as long as he did not hurt anyone. The world seemed to want him to be perfect, and nobody is perfect.

The controversies only seemed to fuel Michael's drive on the court. He won his third NBA MVP in 1991–92, and the Bulls breezed through the regular season and the playoffs. In the NBA Finals, Chicago brushed aside the Portland Trail Blazers to win their second straight championship. This time, the final game took place at home in the Chicago

Stadium. Long after the game ended, Michael led his teammates out of the locker room and into a sea of thousands of fans still in the Stadium. Michael stood on a table and did a victory dance before the screaming, jubilant Chicago fans.

A year later, people thought the Bulls were on the downswing and the Phoenix Suns would knock them off. But Charles Barkley and the Suns went quietly in the finals as the Bulls won

After winning the 1992 Finals, Michael, Scottie Pippen (left), and B. J. Armstrong (right) led the cheers at the Chicago Stadium.

Michael, Scottie, and Bill Cartwright (center) celebrate the Bulls' "three-peat" championship in 1993.

their third straight title. No team had won as many championships in a row since the Boston Celtics won eight straight (1959–66).

Who would have thought that the last game of the 1993 finals would be the end of Michael's career? But in October, Michael walked away from the game. The Bulls then had to learn to go on without him. They were clearly a poorer team in 1993–94, but still one of the best in the league.

☆ ☆ ☆

In March 1994, Michael showed up in Sarasota, Florida, for spring training with the Chicago White Sox. The world's media also descended on Sarasota to witness the greatest living athlete trying a new game. From the start, it was clear that Michael had the athletic tools to be a baseball player. He had the speed to steal dozens of bases, and he had an incredible arm in the outfield. But hitting a baseball is an extremely difficult skill that requires years of constant practice. Michael knew he would need a lot of work before he could even consider the major leagues.

Michael was assigned to the Sox AA minor-league team in Birmingham, Alabama, where he played the entire 1994 season. It was a strange transition. In the NBA, he had grown accustomed to traveling by chartered planes and sleeping in the best hotels. Minor-league baseball meant long bus trips and cheap motels. Michael made things more comfortable for himself and his teammates when he bought a luxury bus for road trips.

SOX
45

☆ ☆ ☆

Throughout his rookie season as a pro baseball player, Michael continually reminded people that he was doing this just for the sake of doing it — so he could say that he'd tried. He had achieved everything he possibly could in basketball. He had retired on top rather than playing while his skills declined and his body aged.

Now he had taken on a new challenge, a sentimental one. When Michael was a boy, he and his father loved talking about baseball. Some of Michael's most treasured childhood memories were of his Little League days and his dad watching him from the stands. Each night, when he took the field as a Birmingham Baron, Michael was concentrating on hitting and fielding and baserunning. But he also was thinking about his father. He was imagining how proud his dad would be to see him playing pro baseball.

Chronology

1963 – Michael Jeffrey Jordan is born on February 17 to Delores and James Jordan in Brooklyn, New York.

1978 – Michael is cut from the varsity basketball team at Laney High School in Wilmington, North Carolina.

1981 – After averaging 23 points per game at Laney High School, Michael accepts a basketball scholarship to play for Dean Smith at the University of North Carolina.

1982 – Michael hits "The Shot" to help North Carolina win the NCAA title in his freshman year.

1983 – Michael is named *The Sporting News* College Player of the Year and leads the U.S. national basketball team to a gold medal at the Pan-Am Games in Venezuela.

1984 – Michael again is named *The Sporting News* College Player of the Year. After a three-year college career (averaging 17.7 points), he enters the NBA Draft. The Chicago Bulls choose Michael with the third pick of the draft. Michael wins a gold medal as part of the U.S. basketball team at the Summer Olympic Games in Los Angeles, California.

1985 – Michael wins the NBA Rookie of the Year award and the Schick award for all-around contributions to a team's success. He is voted by fans to start in the NBA All-Star Game. As a rookie, he leads the Bulls in scoring, rebounding, and assists.

1986 – Michael injures his foot and misses 64 games. He then returns to lead Bulls to the playoffs and sets a playoff scoring record with 63 points in one game; he averages 43.7 points in the playoffs.

1987 – Michael wins his first of seven consecutive scoring titles by averaging 37.1 points (his career high). He also wins the All-Star Game slam-dunk competition.

1988 – Michael wins the NBA Most Valuable Player and Defensive Player of the Year awards — the first time anyone has won both honors. He is named to the All-NBA first team and the NBA All-Defensive first team. In the All-Star Game, Michael scores a record 40 points and wins the All-Star Game MVP award.

1989 – Michael wins his third consecutive scoring title and is given the Schick award for the second time. His last-second shot defeats Cleveland in the second round of the playoffs. Michael marries Juanita Vanoy on September 2 in Las Vegas, Nevada.

1990 – Michael leads the NBA both in minutes played and scoring for the fourth straight season; he also leads the league in steals. He is named to the All-NBA first team for the fourth straight season and the NBA All-Defensive team for the third straight season.

1991 – Michael wins his second NBA MVP award. He leads the Bulls to their first NBA championship as they beat the Los Angeles Lakers in the NBA Finals. Michael is named the NBA Finals MVP.

1992 – Michael wins his third and last NBA MVP award, his sixth straight scoring title, and his second Olympic gold medal. The Bulls repeat as NBA champs, defeating the Portland Trail Blazers. Michael wins the NBA Finals MVP for the second year in a row.

1993 – Michael ties an NBA record by winning his seventh straight scoring title. He is named to the All-NBA first team for the seventh straight season and the NBA All-Defensive first team for the sixth straight season.

– Michael averages 41.0 points in the NBA Finals and captures his third straight NBA Finals MVP. The Bulls win their third straight NBA title, beating the Phoenix Suns.

– James Jordan, Michael's father, is reported to have been murdered.

– On October 6, Michael announces his retirement from pro basketball at age 31. At the time of his retirement, he holds the NBA records for highest scoring average in the regular season (32.3), the All-Star Game (22.1), and the playoffs (34.7).

1994 – Michael becomes a professional baseball player. He plays the 1994 season for the Birmingham Barons, the White Sox AA minor-league team, compiling these statistics: .202 batting average, 3 home runs, 51 runs batted in, 30 stolen bases.

Michael Jeffrey Jordan

Date of Birth: February 17, 1963
Place of Birth: Brooklyn, New York
Height: 6 feet, 6 inches
Home: Highland Park, Illinois
College: University of North Carolina
Pro Teams: Chicago Bulls (basketball), 1984–1993; Birmingham Barons (baseball), 1994
Won NBA MVP Award: 1988, 1991, 1992

PROFESSIONAL CAREER

Season	Team	Scoring Average	Rebounds	Assists	Steals
1984–85	Chicago	28.2	534	481	196
1985–86	Chicago	22.7	64	53	37
1986–87	Chicago	**37.1**	430	377	236
1987–88	Chicago	**35.0**	449	485	**259**
1988–89	Chicago	**32.5**	652	650	234
1989–90	Chicago	**33.6**	565	519	**227**
1990–91	Chicago	**31.5**	492	453	223
1991–92	Chicago	**30.1**	511	489	182
1992–93	Chicago	**32.6**	522	428	**221**
Totals (9 seasons)		32.3	4,219	3,935	1,815

(**Boldface** indicates led league)

About the Author

Philip Brooks grew up near Chicago and rooted for the Bulls for years before Michael Jordan joined the team. Any hopes of a pro basketball career ended when Philip stopped growing at 5-foot-9, and he realized he had no speed and could not jump. Instead, he earned a B.A. from Lake Forest College and an M.F.A. from the University of Iowa Writers' Workshop. His short fiction has appeared in numerous journals, and he has written several children's books for Franklin Watts. Philip and his wife reside in Columbus, Ohio.

8 96